Welcome to The Giggle Club

D1102412

The Giggle Club is a collection of picture books made to put a giggle into early reading. There are funny stories about a contrary mouse, a dancing fox, a turtle with a trumpet, a pig with a ball, a hungry monster, a wide-mouthed frog, an elephant who sneezes away the jungle and lots more! Each of these characters is a member of **The Giggle Club**, but anyone can join: just pick up a **Giggle Club** book, read it and get giggling!

Turn to the checklist on the inside back cover and check off the Giggle Club books you have read.

TEE HEE!

HA HA!

For Marily
P. R.

To my great-nephew
Bart, with love
H. C.

MEOW MONDAY

written by
Phyllis Root

illustrated by
Helen Craig

WALKER BOOKS
AND SUBSIDIARIES
LONDON · BOSTON · SYDNEY

One Monday,
Bonnie Bumble's pussy-willows
all burst into bloom.

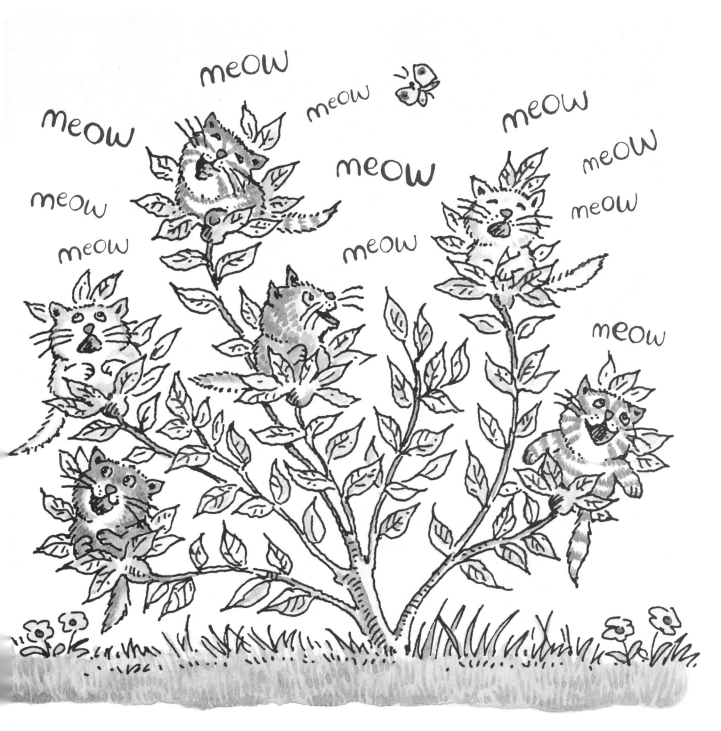

They raised such a rumpus
the hen stopped laying.

The cow wouldn't
give milk.

And the pig and the sheep
covered their ears.

"This rumpus can't go on!"
said Bonnie Bumble.

meOW
meOW
meOW
meOW
meOW

She fed the pussy-willows
cat food and catnip.

She petted them
and brushed them.

She gave them a ball of wool.
But nothing worked.

At last Bonnie remembered
the milk-weed growing
beside the barn.

It was just what the pussy-willows wanted.

purrrr

Purr

purr

Purr

Purrrrr

purrr

Pur

Purrrrr
Purr
purrr
purr
rr
purrr
Purrrrr
purr
purrrr
Purr

When they were full,
the pussy-willows all
curled up for a catnap.

It was so peaceful
the hen laid an egg.

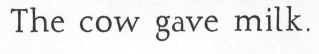

The cow gave milk.

And the pig
and the sheep
uncovered their ears.

"Quiet at last,"
sighed Bonnie Bumble.

And it was ...

until the dogwood started to bloom.

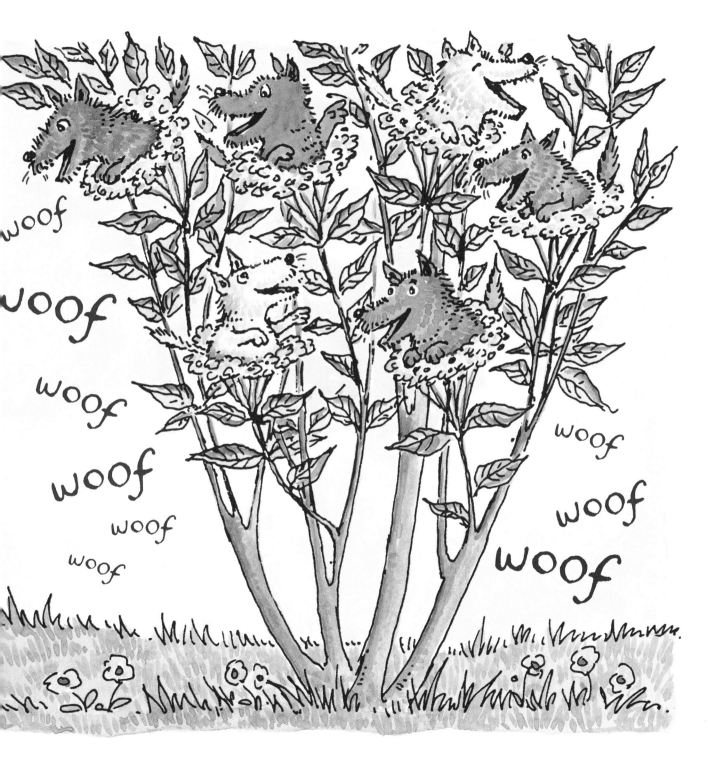

First published 2000 by Walker Books Ltd
87 Vauxhall Walk, London SE11 5HJ

10 9 8 7 6 5 4 3 2 1

Text © 2000 Phyllis Root
Illustrations © 2000 Helen Craig

This book has been typeset in
Calligraphic Antique.

Printed in Hong Kong

British Library Cataloguing in
Publication Data
A catalogue record for this book is
available from the British Library.

ISBN 0-7445-5676-7 (hb)
ISBN 0-7445-7331-9 (pb)

woof
wo

of